THE LITTLE
GREY
DONKEY

HELEN
CRESSWELL

ILLUSTRATED BY
JASON COCKCROFT

Hodder
Children's
Books

A division of Hodder Headline plc

Text copyright © 1965 by Helen Rowe
Illustrations copyright © 1998 by Jason Cockcroft

First published in Great Britain in 1965
by Oliver & Boyd, Ltd.

First published 1998
by Hodder Children's Books

This paperback edition published by
Hodder Children's Books in 1998

A Catalogue record for this book is available from the British Library

ISBN 0 340 70451 9

Printed and bound in Great Britain by Clays Ltd, St Ives plc

Hodder Children's Books
A Division of Hodder Headline plc
338 Euston Road
London NW1 3BH

In loving memory
of L.B.R. - my 'other father'

CONTENTS

Pietro 9

Modestine 16

A Surprise 27

A Lucky Day 36

Amanda 45

Amanda and the Police 53

Amanda Disappears 62

The Search 73

Surprises for Everyone 81

CHAPTER ONE

PIETRO

IN THE MEDITERRANEAN SEA THERE IS a little island called Ibiza. The sun is hot there, so the reddish soil is dry and baked to a fine powder, and the only green is that of the vines and olives on the slopes of the hills. Even this green is pale and dusty, as if it had been faded by the sun. The peasant folk who toil in the fields wear long black clothes to shield themselves from the glare, and when the sun is overhead they drop their tools and lie in the shade, their straw hats tilted down over their faces.

On the south side of the island is the
fine city of Ibiza. It is built on a steep hill
rising from the sea, and at the top, astride
the town, are the great cathedral and the
castillo, or castle. Below them lies the
ancient city, like a warren burrowed in
white stone. You can easily lose your way
in the maze of cobbled alley-ways and steep
stone steps.

Ibiza is a city of whiteness. Everywhere
you look is white, every stone of every
house. In the daytime the whiteness reflects
the glare of the sun and floods even the
shade with a golden light. But at night,
when the moon is out, the whiteness turns
to a pale, unearthly blue, and seems to
glow with a faint light of its own. The city
gleams in the dark. Nothing stirs. Only the
alley cat stalks his own shadow. It is as if the
moonlight makes its own silence.

In one of those cobbled streets a small
boy called Pietro lived with his mother
and his grandfather. When Pietro was a

baby his father had died, and so he did not remember him at all. The family was not a rich one, and Pietro's mother and grand-father both worked hard to keep him clothed and fed. His mother embroidered, sitting for hours with her eyes intent upon the tiny stitches. During the siesta, while others were asleep and Ibiza shimmered in the midday heat, she took her chair into the shady doorway and sat there sewing till the school bell rang.

Grandfather had quite another job. He had a little donkey, Modestine, with a grey coat and long flyaway ears, who pulled a high wooden cart with enormous wheels. Each day early in the morning they went to the market and delivered fruit and vegetables to be shops. Later in the day after the siesta, when the streets were shadowy and cool, they would make their rounds again, collecting the empty boxes and barrels and returning them to the market. It was a good life, and Grandfather was well content.

Pietro went to school, but in the holidays he would go with Grandfather on his rounds. It was his job to see that Modestine was fed and watered and that her thick coat was brushed.

'I shall be doing your work one day, Grandfather,' Pietro would say, 'so I may as well learn now.'

'Ach!' Grandfather would shake his head. 'You will not work with Modestine,

my boy. You are too clever. You have been
to school and know how to read and write.
You will have important work to do. In a
bank, perhaps.'

Grandfather's eyes lit up. He thought
banks were the most important places in

the world – after churches, of course.

'No,' said Pietro. 'You're wrong. I'll never work indoors while there's work to be done outside. Besides, Modestine and I have an agreement.'

'You will change your mind,' Grandfather would say. 'You'll see, you'll see.'

And this is how the argument always ended, with each of them knowing the other might be right.

You may think that life was very slow in Ibiza, and that nothing exciting ever happened in Pietro's life. But you do not need to live in a big modern city to find excitement, and one day something happened that led to a whole train of adventures for Pietro and Modestine.

It was a hot day in June and Pietro nimbly picked his way down the stony street towards home, thinking mainly of the cold orange drink his mother would have ready for him. When he reached the top of

his own street he knew at once that something had happened. A group of women
were standing round his mother's door,
their voices raised shrilly. Pietro quickened
his step. He pushed his way through the
black skirts of the women and saw his
mother's face. She had been crying.

'Mother, Mother, what is it?' He threw
his arms round her.

'Oh, Pietro,' she said, 'it's your
grandfather.'

'What's wrong with him?' asked Pietro.
'Where is he?'

He could feel his heart thudding under
his thin shirt, but in front of these women
he acted like a man.

'He's hurt, Pietro. He's in hospital. And
he won't be home for a long time.'

CHAPTER TWO

MODESTINE

GRANDFATHER'S ACCIDENT WAS A serious one. He had fallen headlong down a flight of steps and hurt his back.

For more than a month he lay in his narrow hospital bed and each day Pietro visited him with fruit and flowers and the news of the town.

Nothing was said to Pietro by either his mother or his grandfather, but he knew money was getting very short. He noticed that his mother gave herself only a small

16

helping at meal times, and that she sat much longer at her needlework.

Grandfather was carving wooden figures as he lay in bed, to sell to the tourists. Pietro wanted to do something to help too, but he knew he must wait until the holidays began.

Two days before school closed, Grandfather was brought home. It was a joyful occasion and everyone in the street came out and clapped and called as he was wheeled up in his special chair. Pietro had led Modestine to the door of their house because he had not heard her master's voice for more than a month, and was pining for him.

'Ah, my little Modestine!' cried Grandfather in delight when he saw her.

He was so delighted that he was tempted to try to rise in order to go to her. But he thought better of it. In any case, there was no need. At the sound of her master's voice the little grey donkey jerked her bridle from Pietro's grasp and went straight to Grandfather, pushing her furry face right into his and stamping her hooves in a kind of tap dance on the cobbles.

'Bravo!' cried a neighbour. 'She has not forgotten you then, eh?'

'Forgotten me!' cried Grandfather

indignantly. 'Forgotten me! Would the sun forget to rise? Forgotten me indeed!'

And he buried his face in Modestine's neck to hide the pleased smile that she had been so glad to see him.

When the neighbours had gone away and left the family alone in the shadowy kitchen, Pietro decided that now was the time to speak his plan. 'The day after tomorrow the holidays begin,' he said.

'Yes, yes,' said Grandfather. 'You'll miss your little jaunts with Modestine and me, my boy. You won't know what to do with yourself.'

'I will, though!' cried Pietro, bursting now to tell his plan.

'Look, Mother, look, Grandfather, Modestine and I know every place you call at, every shop and every stall. We could do your rounds in our sleep. Why shouldn't Modestine and I take on your work? And by the end of the holiday you'll be well again and can do it yourself. What do you say?'

His grandfather looked at Pietro's mother, and she looked back at him. Neither wanted to be the first to speak. They both knew that they needed the money badly, but they were not sure that Pietro could do the work alone. Grandfather was the first to speak.

'It's a good idea,' he said, 'and I'm proud of you for it, Pietro. But there are certain difficulties that I can see.'

'What are they?' demanded Pietro.

'The first, and greatest one,' said Grandfather, 'is the customers. By now they will have found someone else to carry their goods for them. Don't forget that I have already been away for more than a month. And in any case, they may not want to trust a boy.'

'I'll go and talk to them,' said Pietro. 'They're kind-hearted and they like you. They'll let me do it for your sake. What other difficulties are there?'

'Modestine,' said Grandfather.

'Modestine?' said Pietro in surprise.

'Modestine,' repeated Grandfather. 'A donkey is a very strange animal, my boy. No one can read the mind of a donkey.'

'But Modestine knows me well enough,' said Pietro, laughing. 'Think how many times we've all been together on your rounds.'

'Together, yes,' agreed Grandfather. 'But not you and Modestine alone. A donkey knows her own master, Pietro, and to her you are only a friend.'

Pietro's face grew serious. He could see what his grandfather meant, and the thought worried him. But he would not give up easily.

'If Modestine will work with me, will you let me try the rounds?' he asked.

There was a silence and again his grand-father and his mother looked at each other.

'Yes,' said Mother at last. 'I think you should try.'

'Bravo!' cried Grandfather. 'I think so

too. It will be good for you, and good for
Modestine too. She'll grow lazy kicking her
heels all day long without a care in the
world except to flick the flies away.'

After supper, when Mother and Grandfather were sitting in the doorway chatting
to neighbours, Pietro slipped away. He
went to the stall where Modestine was kept
and opened the door. As always, she
seemed glad to see him. She rubbed against
him and stamped her feet. But this was not
enough for Pietro. Would she obey him?

He led her out into the yard to where
the cart had stood unused for more than
a month. Modestine looked at it with
displeasure. She had almost forgotten about
the cart. Gently Pietro turned her round
and tried to back her between the shafts.
This was a job his grandfather usually did.
Pietro only helped to fasten the harness
afterwards.

Modestine trotted firmly forwards again,
away from the cart.

'Come, Modestine,' said Pietro firmly.
He intended to show her who was master.
He tugged at her bridle. Modestine moved
not an inch. He tugged harder. She would
not budge.

Red in the face, Pietro let go of the bridle
and began to tug the cart forwards by the
shafts to where she stood. It was very heavy
and hard work. In the end he managed to
pull the cart so that Modestine was standing

between the shafts. He grasped with relief and set it down. At that moment Modestine trotted forwards again and turned her head to look at Pietro as if to say, 'Who's clever now?'

Pietro groaned. He tried again. For nearly two hours he struggled alone in the little courtyard. He tried coaxing, he tried commanding, he tried trickery, he tried every means he knew. But it was no use. Modestine did not choose to draw the cart, and that was the end of it.

At last it began to grow dark and Pietro knew that he must go home. He led Modestine to her stable and gave her the usual food and water, because it was no use being angry with her and paying her out for refusing to obey him. Grandfather had been right. No one can read the mind of a donkey.

Usually as he went home in the evenings Pietro noticed the stars dangling out over the bay, and the heavy perfume in

the air, and the reflection of the ships'
lights in the water. But tonight he went
with his head down, his feet kicking hard
at the stones and his hands pushing deep in
his pockets. His heart was heavy because he
was afraid Grandfather had been right after
all, and his plan was impossible. He kicked
his way home as crossly as any donkey.

CHAPTER THREE

A SURPRISE

NEXT MORNING PIETRO'S MOTHER went up to the hospital alone to see the doctors there. Pietro stayed at home with Grandfather and tried to be very gay and funny and to make him laugh. But all the while Grandfather was watching him carefully, and in the end he said, 'What's the matter, boy? What are you hiding?'

'Oh, Grandfather,' Pietro blurted out, glad to tell someone of his feelings. 'It's Modestine. She won't draw the cart.'

'It is as I thought,' said Grandfather.
'Don't take it to heart.'

'But my plan!' cried Pietro. 'I was going
to work so hard and earn so much money
to help the family!'

'I know, I know,' nodded Grandfather.
'It's a great pity. Perhaps you can try again?'

'I will try,' said Pietro glumly. 'But
Modestine's obstinate. She's as obstinate as
a – as a donkey!' he ended, and they both
burst out laughing.

When Pietro's mother came from the
hospital he could tell at once that something was wrong. She shook her fist at
Grandfather, pretending to be angry, but
really she was close to tears.

'You are obstinate and foolish,' she
cried. 'Why didn't you tell us the truth?
I knew you were keeping something from
me.'

Grandfather spread his hands and
shrugged.

'I thought perhaps it might make you

worried,' he said. 'I didn't want to worry you.'

'What is it?' asked Pietro. 'What hasn't he told us?'

'You may as well know,' said his mother. 'Your grandfather will never be able to walk again, unless we can find the money to pay a special doctor to come and cure him. That's what. And to think you have known all this time and haven't told us!'

She ran to Grandfather and took his hand, stroking his head gently. Pietro did not know what to say. Did she really mean that Grandfather would never again go with Modestine to the market, would never again move from his chair? Tears stung his eyes. He turned and dashed through the door, hardly knowing where he was going.

He found himself at last at Modestine's stall. He threw himself against her thick grey coat and sobbed as if his heart would break. Modestine stood patiently, every now and then turning her head and nuzzling him as though to comfort him. After a while he felt better. He took hold of Modestine by both long ears and turned her head towards him, so that he looked right into her large brown eyes. She gazed back without a flicker.

'Listen, Modestine,' said Pietro. 'You've got to help me. Listen!'

And he told Modestine the whole story
of his grandfather, and how they needed
her to work for them so that they could
earn enough to have a doctor to make him
well again. When he had finished he gave
her ears a final gentle pull.

'Do you understand, Modestine? Do
you?' he pleaded. The donkey took a few
paces forwards. She seemed to be trying to
move the latch of the stable door with her
nose. Puzzled, Pietro lifted the latch so that
the door stood half open, and watched.
Modestine pushed the door open and
trotted out into the yard. She looked about
her and then, seeing what she was looking
for, gave a little toss of her head and trotted
forwards again.

Pietro gave a cry of gladness and
astonishment.

She had gone of her own accord and
was standing patiently between the shafts
of the cart waiting to be harnessed. He ran
to her and threw his arms round her neck.

'Oh, Modestine!' he cried. 'You *did* understand!' Excitedly he fastened her harness, thinking all the while that what his grandfather had said was true. You certainly cannot read the mind of a donkey.

Then they drove out into the hot midday sun. It was good to be on the cart again with Modestine carefully placing her feet on the smooth cobbles, even though Grandfather was not there to share it with them. Many families were sitting in their doorways and they all called greetings to him as he passed. He was proud to be the master of a donkey and cart.

At their own house Pietro stopped and shouted, 'Holloa! Come out and see what's here!'

His mother came to the door.

'Gracious!' she cried. 'What has happened? Grandfather told me that Modestine was shirking.'

'She's not now!' cried Pietro triumphantly.

A Surprise

'What's happening?' his grandfather
called from inside the house.

'Go and fetch him!' whispered Pietro.
'Let him see!'

So mother went in and wheeled
Grandfather to the door in his chair. He
was astonished too, but tried not to show it.

'Well, Modestine,' he said, 'so you're
going to be good, after all.' He stretched
out his hand and the donkey moved
towards him.

'How did you do it?' asked Grand–
father. 'Did you have ten strong men to
help you to drag her between the shafts?'

'She did it of her own free will,' said
Pietro. He did not say a word about
telling Modestine the story, and yet he
had a strange feeling that his grandfather
understood.

'Well,' said Pietro happily, 'that's
settled then. Tomorrow Modestine and
I will start work, and soon you'll be
well and working again. Do I smell my
dinner?'

He jumped down and hitched
Modestine to the ring in the stone wall.
He went inside and sat down to wait.

And as he looked about him it seemed
that never had the stone pitchers in rows
on the floor looked so clean and round

and friendly, and never had the flowers on
the bleached wooden table looked so
upright and alive.

Through the open door he could see
the sunlight flooding the shadow with gold,
and best of all he could see Modestine's
long, pointed ears, standing out like wings.
Then his mother put his bowl before him,
wreathed with savoury steam. Pietro
decided that life was perfect.

CHAPTER FOUR

A LUCKY DAY

EARLY NEXT MORNING PIETRO TOOK Modestine to the market. He was full of excitement. As they went down the steep hill he caught glimpses of the dawn reflected in the bay in a huge blaze, and he felt how good it was to be with the day from the very beginning.

When they reached the vast square of the old city Pietro could hear voices shouting, and boxes and barrels being moved.

Modestine trotted through the great

arch and down the long
ramp into the lower part of the city.

It was a familiar sight and Pietro
drank it in eagerly, forgetting for a
moment that he had work to do. He
noticed the huge, glowing piles of fruit,
the grapes, olives, melons, bananas, oranges,
peaches, and he sniffed in the sharp tang
of the mingled fruits and vegetables. Under
the sackcloth awnings Pietro caught sight of
Señor Justino, a friend of Grandfather's.

'Ah, Pietro my boy,' cried Señor Justino,
shaking him by the hand. 'Up early, eh?
And how's poor Grandfather? Getting
better?'

'Getting better,' agreed Pietro.

'Ah, good, good. I must get on with my
work. Take a banana for yourself, my boy –
take any fruit you want. It's your holiday,
isn't it? Enjoy your self and give my best
wishes to your grandfather.'

He was going to walk away, but Pietro
caught him by the sleeve.

'Señor Justino,' he said, 'wait a minute, please. I want to explain. I have come to the market because I'm taking over Grandfather's work until he is better again.'

Señor Justino looked down at him in astonishment.

'Eh?' he exclaimed in a loud voice. 'Eh?'

'I know all the rounds, señor,' said Pietro rapidly, 'and I'm willing to work hard. Won't you let me do your carrying for you?'

Señor Justino scratched his head.

'Does your grandfather say so?' he said at last.

'Oh yes,' replied Pietro. 'I have his approval.'

'Mmmmmm.' Señor Justino fingered his chin as if doing so would help him to solve his problem.

'I already have someone to do my carrying for me,' he said at last. 'I couldn't help it – someone had to do it until your grandfather was better. I would have given him the work again when he was well.'

'Then give it to me!' begged Pietro. 'I'm taking the work in his place, don't you see? It's exactly the same thing.'

Señor Justino's face cleared.

'Yes, it is, isn't it?' he said. 'Then I'll do it. But not today. Today the other carrier will have to do it. Come back tomorrow at the same time.'

'Thank you, thank you!' cried Pietro, and taking Señor Justino's huge brown fist he wrung it hard. 'I'll be here. Thank you!'

The story was the same all round the market, and at the end of the morning Pietro went home with the news that every single one of Grandfather's old customers was ready to employ him.

'Good!' cried Grandfather. 'I am proud of you, Pietro.'

'This afternoon,' said Pietro, 'Modestine and I are going round the town.'

He wanted to show off the little grey donkey to his friends, who would not be up early enough to see them in the morning.

He pinned two rosettes that were usually kept for feast-days to Modestine's harness and set off. It was very hot and the donkey did not hurry.

The only people about were the tourists, who never dreamt of resting in the heat of the day. With red, perspiring faces they toiled up the hill. They looked like gaily coloured tropical birds in their brilliant shirts and cotton dresses, with huge straw hats flapping on their heads. Nearly all of them carried cameras and every now and then would stop and – click, click – the shutters would be working busily.

As Pietro came down towards them the tourists all stared at him.

'Just look at that darling little grey donkey!' cried an American lady in lime-green. 'Say, Harry, get a shot of them both, do!'

'How can I?' growled Harry, fumbling with his leather case. 'By the time I've got this darned thing set up he'll be a mile away.'

The lady in lime-green leapt into the road and held up her arms, like a policeman on point duty. Modestine stopped out of shock before Pietro even had time to tug on the reins.

'Waitee un momento?' asked the American lady, stabbing her finger in the direction of Harry and then pretending to take a photograph, to show Pietro what she meant.

'Certainly, if you wish,' said Pietro pleasantly.

Her mouth fell open.

'You speak English?' she gasped.

'Yes,' said Pietro modestly, 'a little.'

'Well, that's fine,' said the American lady, stepping back out of the road and dropping her arm. 'Would you mind if Harry just took a photo of you and your cute little mule?'

'Donkey,' said Pietro.

'Well, donkey, then,' said the lime-green American.

'Not at all,' said Pietro.

By now dozens of tourists had collected and all were busily clicking their cameras, while Harry fumbled with his.

He managed to take his photograph at last and then, rather sheepishly, pressed a coin into Pietro's hand.

'Thanks, kid,' he said.

Then the other tourist, not to be outdone, all pressed forward to give Pietro something as well. He was quite bewildered by their flocking and twittering, and he only really came to when he found himself all alone again, with his hands full of coins. He counted them up. There were seventy-eight pesetas! One coin was a 25-peseta piece, and he guessed this must be Harry's.

He drove round the city in a dream and he and Modestine must have been photographed a hundred times. And when at last he was home and was emptying his pockets under the astonished gaze of his mother and grandfather, he was almost too dazed to explain how it had all happened. And the three of them sat there and stared at the silvery shower of coins for all the world as if they had been turned to stone.

CHAPTER FIVE

AMANDA

ALL PIETRO'S EARNINGS WENT INTO what the family called 'The Grandfather Fund'. That night Pietro lay awake for a long time thinking hard. Early next morning he crept into Grandfather's room. 'Grandfather!' he whispered.

Grandfather stirred and opened his eyes, looking bright and startled like a squirrel.

'Can I talk to you, Grandfather?' asked Pietro softly.

'At this time in the morning?' said Grandfather.

'It's about the rounds,' explained Pietro.
'I've been thinking. If I have to collect
all the empty crates and barrels in the
evening I shan't be able to go into the
city in the afternoon, because it would
make Modestine too tired. So why don't
I collect the crates and barrels from the day
before, when I go round in the morning
to deliver? Then I can earn pesetas with
Modestine in the afternoon.'

'Marvellous!' exclaimed Grandfather.
'Such reasoning!'

Now, it had occurred to Grandfather
many years ago that it needed only one
round a day to serve his customers just as
well. But Grandfather had many friends,
and the part of the day he enjoyed best
was the evening round when work was
over and there was plenty of time for a
friendly chat. But it would never do to
let Pietro know all this.

'Marvellous!' he said again, as if a veil
had suddenly been drawn from his eyes.

46

'Do you really think so?' asked Pietro.

'I do indeed. You are very clever. Too clever even for a bank,' said Grandfather. 'I shall now go back to sleep. Good luck on your rounds.' And he turned over and closed his eyes.

That day Pietro explained his new plan to all his customers, who were full of admiration. Pietro was delighted.

In the afternoon he drove down with Modestine on to the quayside. The big boat to Palma, Majorca, was soon to set sail and everyone had come down to watch the sight. Pietro was in great demand again with the tourists and his pockets were soon bulging. Modestine basked in her fame and tossed her head and arched her neck as if she were a film star. No one could resist her.

That evening Pietro went down to the quayside again on an errand.

Some fishermen were busy laying out their nets on the stones and mending their gear, and Pietro stopped to watch them.

'Hi. Aren't you the kid with the mule?' said a voice.

'Donkey,' said Pietro, turning.

'O.K., donkey,' said the girl. She was a little taller and older than himself, with silvery hair in a long pony tail. She wore blue jeans and a white cotton shirt and had a brace over her front teeth.

'Yes, I am,' said Pietro.

'Nice job you've got,' said the girl. 'I'm Amanda. Who're you?'

Pietro told her.

'Shake,' she said. So Pietro shook. They stood and looked at each other.

'Are you here on holiday? asked Pietro. She nodded.

'Was,' she said.

'What do you mean? You're still here, aren't you?' said Pietro.

'*I* am,' she said.

Pietro did not know what to make of her. 'What do you mean?' he asked again.

'I'm here, but my family isn't see?' she said. She took a piece of gum from her pocket, offered a piece to Pietro and put one in her own mouth.

'S'right.' She chewed carelessly at her gum as if this sort of thing happened to her twice a week.

'But why?' asked Pietro.

'It was like this, see. We all got on the boat back to Palma, and I got a bit bored. So for a laugh I thought I'd run back down on to the quay and then sort of holler up at Ma and Pa and give 'em a fright. Well, when I got down there, I saw this crowd all peering at something, so I went over to find out what, and it was you and your mule.'

'Donkey,' said Pietro.

'O.K., donkey,' said Amanda. 'Well, I guess I didn't notice them taking up the steps, and I stood on the quay all right and hollered myself hoarse, but they didn't even see me.'

'How terrible!' exclaimed Pietro.

Pietro looked at her in awe. He had never met anyone like this girl before. She seemed afraid of nothing.

'What are you going to do?' he asked.

She shrugged.

'Wait around, I guess. They'll be back.'

'Come home with me,' said Pietro. 'My mother will put you up for the night. You'll be frightened all by yourself.'

'Who's frightened?' She drew herself up straight. 'Not me. No, sir. I'll stay here all night and wait.'

'Don't Amanda,' begged Pietro. 'It's really all my fault in a way. If you hadn't come to look at Modestine, you'd have caught the boat.'

'No, thanks,' said Amanda. But she didn't sound quite so sure this time.

'All right,' he said. 'I should sit behind the bales and wait if I were you. Goodbye!'

'So long!' Amanda stood and watched him go. She was chewing hard.

Pietro turned a corner out of sight and then went into a little cafe on the pavement. He sat under one of the green umbrellas and ordered an orangeade. He drank it slowly. He heard the cathedral clock chime the quarters twice while he sat there. He got up. It was almost dark.

He went back along the quay until he could make out the pile of bales where he had left Amanda. He crept quietly nearer. He heard a few sniffs, and a slow smile spread over his face. He poked his head suddenly round the pile. Amanda squealed. 'Oh! It's you,' she said with a shaky laugh. 'Come on, Amanda, it's getting late,' said Pietro.

This time she did not argue; they turned their backs on the sea and walked together towards the moonlit city.

CHAPTER SIX

AMANDA AND THE POLICE

THE NEXT MORNING PIETRO WAS
wakened by the sound of voices.
Lying in a furry haze he heard the
words, 'Swell, one hundred per cent swell,'
– and remembered Amanda.

Quickly he dressed and went out to
find her helping his mother with the
breakfast.

'You must hurry, Pietro,' his mother
told him. 'Finish your rounds as quickly as
you can, and then you must take Amanda
to the police station. Her mother and

53

father will be very worried. Ah! How worried they will be!'

'They sure will be wondering,' agreed Amanda, stretching out a thin brown arm for a golden-coated roll. 'Wish I didn't have to go to the cops, though. I always seem to be mixed up with the cops, even back home.'

Pietro's mother looked alarmed, but Pietro suspected that Amanda was showing off.

'Don't worry,' he said, 'the cells are not too bad. And they allow bread and water twice a day, not once only. You will be fairly comfortable.' He burst out laughing at the look on her face.

It was a hard job to get Amanda to the police station.

She kept stopping and looking at things and pointing them out to Pietro.

'Look, Pietro. Look at those lovely flowers on that wall. It looks just like a waterfall of purple gushing down!'

'Pietro, how many steps are there up the cathedral? Let's count them.'

'On the way back,' said Pietro firmly. He had used the same tricks himself when his mother used to take him to the dentist.

At the police station Alberto, the chief policeman, nearly embraced them with delight. He had been receiving telephone

 calls all night and his hair was almost upright with worry. He banged the telephone down on its hook after the thousandth and – he hoped – the last call.

'American?' he gasped. 'Amanda Cunnington?'

'That's me,' said Amanda, swinging her pony-tail. 'Don't say you've heard of me?'

'Heard of you?' groaned the superintendent. '*Heeeard* of you?'

His head was ringing with the name.

'Palma,' he muttered, 'I must ring Palma.'

He picked up the phone and started dialling, waving to Amanda and Pietro to sit down.

He asked for the hotel in Palma and then held the telephone a very long way from his ear, which was not a good sign. When Amanda's father began to speak the line spluttered and crackled so that Amanda and Pietro could hear him shouting even from where they sat.

'We have found her, we have found her!' yelled Alberto triumphantly.

'Found me my eye!' muttered Amanda. 'I gave myself up!'

'Here! Right here, señor, sitting in my office, safe and sound!'

The telephone crackled so violently that the policeman was forced to hold it even further from his ear. He nodded and beckoned to Amanda.

'Your dear father wishes to speak with you,' he said, loudly enough for Mr Cunnington in Palma to hear him.

Amanda pulled a face.

'Here goes!' she said to Pietro, and stepped over to the telephone.

'Hi, Pa,' said Amanda timidly. Her voice was so tiny that Pietro hardly heard it.

The telephone almost leapt out of her hand like a tadpole. It throbbed and quivered and spluttered as if it were alive, and did not stop for a full two minutes.

'Yes, Pa,' said Amanda, still in the same tiny voice. This was not the bold bad Amanda of yesterday.

The conversation came to an end at last. Amanda put the receiver back on the hook and sat down suddenly as if her legs were wobbly.

'Well? Well?' asked Alberto excitedly. 'What does he say?'

'Most of it was private,' said Amanda with dignity.

'But what are we to do with you?' the superintendent half shrieked. He wanted to get Amanda off his island as quickly as possible.

'Oh, I'm not going yet,' said Amanda airily.

'N–not going?' he stammered. He too suddenly felt the need to sit down.

'Nope,' said Amanda. 'My pa's coming to get me at the end of the week. He's in Palma on business at the moment and the rest of the family flew back to the States last night.'

'Good,' said Pietro. 'Let's go.'

They started for the door.

'Wait! Wait a moment!' cried Alberto. 'Where are you going?'

'Home,' said Pietro.

'But I haven't got your name and address,' protested Alberto feebly. Pietro waited while he entered his name and address in a lordly black book and then they were free to go.

'I guess I'd better write Pa a letter,' said Amanda as they sauntered along. 'And then I'd like to go for a nice cool swim.'

'You go,' said Pietro. 'I can't.'

'Can't?' She stared at him. 'Why not?'

So Pietro told her the whole story, and

explained how his afternoons were spent earning pesetas for the Grandfather Fund. For once Amanda was serious.

'You mean to say you're going to earn all that money yourself?' she asked. 'Just in your holidays?'

Pietro's face clouded. 'Well,' he said, 'I may not get it all this holiday. But there's next holiday. And the next. I won't give up.'

'I wouldn't either,' said Amanda. 'But I hope it won't take *too* long, Pietro.'

'So do I,' said Pietro miserably. They walked for a while in silence.

'I'll tell you what, Pietro,' said Amanda suddenly and loudly. 'You'll just have to leave it to me.'

Pietro stopped and looked in astonishment at her deadly serious face and thoughtful frown. She really was the oddest girl he had ever met. He burst out laughing.

'Come on, Amanda,' he cried. 'The wind might change and you'll stay like that till the sea dries up. Come on – you've got three more days on Ibiza, and you don't want to waste a single minute!'

CHAPTER SEVEN

AMANDA DISAPPEARS

PIETRO'S MOTHER AND GRAND-
father were glad that Amanda was
staying for a few more days.
Grandfather was glad because Amanda
made him chuckle and Pietro's mother was
glad because it was good to see him
chuckle. As for Pietro, he wanted to hear
all about America, and thought that
Amanda could tell him. Here he was mis-
taken. All his questions were answered by a
swing of silvery hair and either 'Yeah', or
'Nope', and after a minute or so she would

become fidgety and her eyes would stray restlessly in search of some new interest. Pietro could hardly keep up with her. She wanted to leap through Ibiza like a cricket on her thin, sharp-boned legs with her spidery shadow dancing tirelessly after her.

'What's this?' she would say. And before Pietro had time to finish his reply, off she would go again, and he would follow, grumbling.

But in the afternoons, while Pietro and Modestine went down to the city in search of tourists, Amanda would stay behind in the shadow of the house with Grandfather. When Pietro came back they were always there together, both chattering so hard that you would think it was a competition.

'She is a smart one, that girl,' Grand-father would say delightedly. 'Too smart even for a bank.'

And Amanda would swing her mane as if to say, 'Well, of course, though I don't say so myself!'

The three days seemed to pass very
quickly, and on the evening before Mr
Cunnington was to come for Amanda
everyone was very sad. But the sadness
was mixed with pleasure, as so often in
life, by a special happening.

Pietro's mother secretly prepared a
farewell party for Amanda, and as the
custom is in Ibiza, it was held in the street.

Tables were set up and all Amanda's
new friends sat round to eat and drink and
wish her luck.

Even Alberto the worried policeman
was invited, and managed to smile once or
twice, because soon Amanda would be
gone and he could enjoy his siestas again.
As things turned out, he was quite wrong.

Grandfather in his wheelchair sat at the head of the table because he was the master of the house. Amanda sat next to him and at the end of the party made a speech in which she invited him and everyone else in Ibiza to come and stay with her in America whenever they felt like it.

When the party was over Pietro said to Amanda, 'Now let's go and play *Hide for a forfeit* with the others.'

'*Hide and seek*, you mean,' said Amanda.

'*Hide for a forfeit*,' said Pietro firmly. It was a favourite game with the children of Ibiza. One person hides, and if he is not found within a certain time, all the searchers must pay a forfeit. If he is found, then it is he who must pay.

So the children scattered and ran like rabbits through the white warren of Ibiza, up and down the stone steps, through the arches and

over the smooth cobbles.
They played until the
shadows were violet and
the fairy lights began to
pop out on the quayside
below.

'That was a good game,'
said Amanda to Pietro as they
trudged home together. 'I think it has
give me an idea.'

Pietro peered at her, but could not see
her face. 'What kind of idea?' he asked
suspiciously.

'Oh, just an idea,' said Amanda airily.

But somehow the way she said it made
Pietro uneasy. You could never really tell
what she would do next.

Long after they had reached home,
eaten their supper and gone to bed, Pietro
lay awake, and his mind kept returning to
that one remark.

He was just beginning to feel sleepy at
last when he heard a faint clinking noise,

as if two pitchers had been knocked
together. Then there was a soft scrape.
A chair had been moved on the stone floor.
He sat up, wide awake, and listened. Not
another sound was to be heard. He lay
down again, but still be could not sleep.

'I'll see if Amanda is awake,' he decided.
'I'll ask her what she meant by that remark
of hers. Then perhaps I shall have some
sleep.'

He got up and padded over to the door.
Amanda had been sleeping on a mattress in
the living room. He whispered her name
but there was no reply. Nor was there any
sound of breathing. It was very, very still.

Pietro tiptoed back, lit the lamp he kept
by his bedside and then went into the
living room. As he raised the lamp, shadows
swung wildly over the walls and ceiling.
On the floor lay a mattress and a rumpled
heap of rugs. Amanda was not there.
Pietro's heart flew against his ribs.

As his eyes grew used to the light he

saw that lying on the table were two pieces
of paper, gleaming in the dimness. He
placed the lamp on the table and spelled
out his name on the first envelope. On the
second it said, 'For my father.'

'Heaven!' thought Pietro. 'Her father!
What will he say?'

He remembered the telephone that had
danced as if it had been alive, and he
trembled.

He opened his own letter with fingers that suddenly felt fat and fluffy with clumsiness. He peered to read Amanda's spiky writing.

Dear Pietro,

Don't worry, I'm O.K. I'm doing it for Grandfather. When my father comes tomorrow give him the other letter. Then the fun will start!

Your friend,
Amanda

Pietro read the letter three times, each time trying to read a different meaning into it. In vain. The only fact that stood out clearly was that tomorrow he would have to meet Mr Cunnington on the quayside with the news that Amanda was lost again. He groaned and made for the door.

Out in the street the cobbles were washed in moonlight and whole city glowed a bluish white.

Pietro sped barefoot over the stones, which were still dry and warm from the day's heat. He leapt down flights of shadowy steps and sped through zig-zag alleys of shuttered houses. Down he went through the vast arch and on down the ramp into the deserted market. Thin cats ran like ink across the path.

He reached the quay and ran, his chest bursting, through the swing doors into the sudden light and noise of the police head-quarters. He stood drawing breath in huge gasps and saw many faces turned to look at him. In particular he saw Alberto, close by his telephone.

'Oh, quickly!' he gasped. 'It's Amanda! She's disappeared. We must find her! We must!'

The whites of Alberto's eyes stretched like elastic.

'You are joking!' he pleaded, his voice beginning to rise. 'Please, *please*. Say you are joking.'

'I'm not joking! She's gone, I tell you!' cried Pietro. 'Oh, hurry, do hurry!'

'It is too much, 'said Alberto. 'Too much. I resign.'

There was an outbreak of confused voices and suddenly everyone was crowding round Alberto. Patting him and offering advice. Only Pietro stood apart, thinking for the first time not of Mr Cunnington and his angry face, but of Amanda, all alone in the strange, moonlit silence of Ibiza.

CHAPTER EIGHT

THE SEARCH

PIETRO WOULD NEVER FORGET THAT night. He did not go to bed at all. First he ran home and told his grandfather and mother what had happened, and then he went back to join the search.

On second thoughts Alberto had decided not to resign - not, at any rate, until the morning. Instead he sat importantly behind his desk at the headquarters, organising the biggest moonlight search that Ibiza had ever known. The whole of his force was given strict instructions that there should be silence and secrecy.

Wearing their rubber-soled shoes, the men were soon buzzing through the stony honeycomb of passage-ways and alleys in search of the missing Amanda. But the policemen of Ibiza are not able to keep quiet for very long, even when their shoes are made of rubber. They are easily exited by clues such as footprints in the dust, or dropped hair-ribbons. They whisper hoarsely to each other as they go, to keep up with the latest news, and their whispers quickly turn to shouts.

So it was not very long before shutters were flung back and yellow blades of light sliced the shadows. Soon doors opened and groups of people still in their nightclothes stood talking excitedly in the streets. In less than half an hour the whole of Ibiza was wide awake, and the streets were so full of people that it might have been a fiesta. Many of them carried torches, although it was nearly as light as day by now.

The Search

In the middle of the confusion Pietro had a sudden idea, and began to push his way back uphill towards the stall where Modestine would be sleeping in the deep hay.

When he reached the small square he found it deserted. Most of the people had gone below to join the big crowds.

'They don't really care if they find Amanda or not,' thought Pietro bitterly. 'They think it is a game!'

He went into the quiet yard and walked slowly to the stall. He peered in and could make out the shape of the little donkey lying peacefully snoring, her furry ears folded back.

'Modestine!' hissed Pietro. 'Modestine!'

The donkey opened her eyelids a notch but did not budge.

'Get up, Modestine!' urged Pietro. 'It's important.'

Modestine shut her eyes again, so Pietro reached for a long stick and prodded it

sharply in her ribs. She scrambled up,
snorting indignantly at Pietro. Donkeys do
not like to be disturbed when they are
slumbering peacefully. Modestine obviously
felt inclined to be awkward.

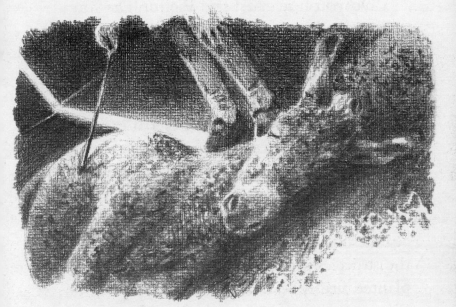

Pietro tugged her from the stall into the
yard. She was still too sleepy to protest,
but she stamped her hooves sharply to
make sparks fly.

'Come on,' said Pietro. 'We must go
and find Amanda.'

Modestine did not stir. She closed her
eyes and seemed quite ready to go to sleep
again standing up.

'Do you hear me?' said Pietro. 'Do you
realise that her father is coming to fetch her
tomorrow? And if she is not there, do you
know who will be blamed? I shall.'

Modestine's head nodded.

'And Grandfather,' added Pietro craftily.

Modestine's eyes were suddenly wide
open. Pietro's heart jumped. I have won,
he thought.

But, oddly enough, Modestine pulled
against him when he tried to lead her into
the street. She stood with her hooves
planted firmly so that however hard
Pietro tugged and strained, she did not
stir one inch.

'Very well!' he cried angrily, throwing
down the rein. 'If you won't help, you
won't! Who'd have a donkey!'

Modestine immediately turned and trotted back into her stall, but Pietro did not even wait to see her go. He slammed out of the little courtyard and ran down the alley. As he went he could hear Modestine braying, but he took no notice. Suddenly he turned a corner and ran right into a crowd of people.

'Oho!' they cried when they saw him. 'Here is Pietro – let's ask him. Pietro, where do you think the American girl is hiding? And why has she run away at all?'

'I don't know,' said Pietro crossly. 'Perhaps she thinks it's a joke.'

'A joke?' said the policeman who was leading the band. 'A joke? When it gives the superintendent grey hairs and keeps a whole city out of bed at night?'

'Leave the boy alone,' said a voice, and the crowd parted to make a path for Grandfather in his wheelchair.

'It's not Pietro's fault,' he said quietly. 'Amanda left a note for him on the table before she went, and she says that what she is doing, she is doing for my sake.'

The crowd stood silent. They did not know what to say.

'I don't pretend to understand,' admitted Grandfather. 'But that is a good girl. A good girl – and clever. That is why I think we should all go quietly to our homes and wait until the morning.'

The policeman placed himself squarely at the head of his band. 'I have my orders to carry out,' he said firmly. 'I respect your wishes, but orders are orders.'

Grandfather nodded as if to say, 'That is true.'

'On with the search!' roared the crowd delightedly. And off they pranced, waving their torches like shock-headed shrimps of light.

CHAPTER NINE

SURPRISES FOR EVERYONE

AT DAWN THE WEARY PEOPLE OF Ibiza began to make their way home. The sun crackled and leapt over the harbour with promises of a brilliant day. The boat from Majorca was due at nine o'clock and everyone went for breakfast before going down to the quayside to see the fun that was bound to take place.

The whole of Ibiza was down by the quay. The police had a hard job to keep the crowds back from the dais they had erected so that everyone could have a good view of the proceedings.

One person was missing, but no one seemed to notice. Alberto, the super-intendent of police, had quietly slipped away half an hour ago. He had been seized by sudden panic at the thought of facing Mr Cunnington and had decided that an arrest must be made at all costs. At least then no one could suggest that he had been idle.

It had taken him a long while to make up his mind just whom he ought to arrest. He had toyed with the idea of several people, from the Captain of the *Majorca Queen* who had sailed off without Amanda, to Pietro himself, who should have kept a better eye on her. Then he had had a sudden, brilliant flash of inspiration that had sent him scurrying up the steep hill of Ibiza like a madman.

'Quickly!' he kept muttering under his breath. 'Quickly! There is no time to lose.'

Pietro, down at the quay, knew nothing of this. He kept raising his eyes to the *castillo* and the olive-covered slopes beyond as if expecting a miracle.

Already the steamer was in the bay, and as it drew up alongside, white paint sparkling in the sun, a great burst of music filled the air. It was the band of Ibiza, sitting on wooden chairs with their ankles crossed and solemnly blowing and scraping their shabby instruments.

83

The captain of the ship looked delighted, thinking that this reception was in his honour. The gang-plank was lowered and he began to descend, followed by a tall, thin man in a white suit, who could only be Mr Cunnington.

Pietro gulped, and stepped forward, the letter tightly clasped. He dared not look up, but stood staring at the middle button on the American's jacket. The band stopped suddenly in the middle of their tune, and the silence was enormous. You could hear the mosquitoes, and the gurgling of water under the quay. Quiet. Quiet.

Then the miracle happened.

The silence was shattered by a loud clattering of hooves and feet on the cobbles, and a rough braying of an outraged Modestine, and – miracle of miracles – by the sobs and shrieks of a furious Amanda. Pietro felt the gooseflesh prickling up and down his spine. He hardly dared look.

Just coming on to the quay was Alberto, his face lobster-red and twitching with pride. With one pudgy hand he tugged at Modestine, coat on end and spiky with indignation. With the other he half dragged a red-eyed, stamping Amanda, clothes and hair stuck with straw like a porcupine.

The crowds opened their mouths like a vast, silent choir at a sign from an invisible conductor. Silently they drew aside to let the trio pass. Alberto's heavy breathing seemed to fill the whole square. He bowed to Mr Cunnington.

'Your daughter, señor,' he gasped – but with dignity.

Amanda threw herself at her father and clasped him round the waist. How the crowd cheered! The goats on the vine-covered terraces stopped chewing and gazed down at the scene, hiccoughing mildly in astonishment.

Pietro threw his arms round Modestine's neck.

'You found her!' he cried. 'Oh, Modestine, you found her!'

'I object!' roared Alberto. His voice had returned. '*I* found her. This donkey is an accessory to the crime. I go up to the animal's stall to arrest the creature, and what do I find? Both of them, hiding in the hay.'

'We were *not* hiding!' Amanda shouted. 'We were asleep. I was there all night, but you were too stupid to look. Modestine tried to tell Pietro that I was there, but he wouldn't listen. How dare you try to arrest her? And now, you – you – you *bumbling* policeman, you've spoilt everything, and Grandfather won't be able to walk again, and it's all your fault!'

The crowd gasped, and Alberto began
to fill and empty his cheeks with air in his
distress.

'Would someone explain to me just
what is going on?' said Mr Cunnington,
who was removing a violet silk hand-
kerchief from his breast pocket to lend to
Amanda, whose cheeks were wet again.

Amanda poured out the whole story
in between her sobs. She had been playing
Hide for a forfeit with her father. If she
had won, her father was to have given
the money for Grandfather to have his
operation.

The crowd went mad with admiration.
They forgot that they had been up all night
looking for her. Grandfather in his wheelchair was pushed forward to join the group
by the gang-plank, and Amanda and Pietro
ran to him.

Gradually the crowd quietened and
waited for what was to happen next. Mr
Cunnington beckoned to a grey-haired

gentleman in a grey linen suit who had
been standing behind him all the while.
He bowed to Grandfather.

'May I present Dr Matthew Sylvester?'
he said. 'I think he will be able to help
you.'

Amanda's hand flew to her mouth.
'Hey, Pop!' she said. 'You were going to
help him anyway!'

'You told me the situation in your
letter,' said her father. 'It was the least I
could do. Particularly as these kind people
have put up with you for three whole days.'

It is no use even trying to describe what
happened after that. The whole city was in
a state of delight. Just think – Alberto, the
superintendent of police, had even made a
speech in which he apologised for arresting
Modestine.

'The donkey is a genius,' he admitted
handsomely. 'That much is obvious.'

Almost everyone made a speech.
Amanda made one thanking Pietro and

Modestine; Mr Cunnington made one,
thanking Alberto and Pietro's family;
Grandfather made one, thanking everyone
on the whole island. The little grey donkey
herself would have given a speech if he had
been able. As it was, she merely brayed
once and loudly, and the crowd clapped her
till their hands were tingling.

That night there were fireworks, and the white stones of Ibiza were lit with a thousand colours. Pietro and Amanda didn't go to bed until the last spark had fallen, dwindled and died over the dark waters of the bay. Modestine slept in her deep hay with the long, snoring breath of a very contended donkey. And the moon came out, now that the fireworks were over, bringing its blue magic to the white city of Ibiza.

THE LITTLE SEA HORSE

Helen Cresswell

Out of the sea comes an enchanted creature –
a tiny horse of purest white with hooves of
brightest gold.

Molly knows he is far too precious to keep,
but the local townspeople lock the magical
horse in a cage, and throw away the key.
Only Molly can find a way to release him
back to the sea.

A lyrical and deeply evocative tale from a
magical storyteller.

Another Story Book from Hodder Children's Books

THE SEA PIPER

Helen Cresswell

Every day Harriet's father is out at sea with the shrimping fleet, while she hunts for shrimps in the deep rock pools. Until one day, suddenly, there are no shrimps. Something, or someone, has magicked them away.

Out collecting shells one pale, misty morning, Harriet meets a stranger – the mysterious sea piper. Perhaps he holds the key? If only Harriet can persuade him to help . . .

THE DRAGON'S CHILD

Jenny Nimmo

'Mother, I'm falling.'
With a final squeal, the dragon's child slid
from his mother's back and fell earthwards
through the wind.

Dando the dragon child must now survive alone. In a place where the dreadful Doggins lurk. Only an orphaned slave girl offers him hope. She knows he is a magical creature, and their special friendship keeps them both safe, for now . . .

By the Smarties Prize winning author of *The Snow Spider*.

ORDER FORM

0 340 63461 8   THE LITTLE SEA HORSE   £3.50
Helen Creswell

0 340 68285 X   THE SEA PIPER   £3.50
Helen Creswell

0 340 67304 4   THE DRAGON'S CHILD   £3.50
Jenny Nimmo

All Hodder Children's books are available at your local bookshop or newsagent, or can be ordered direct from the publisher. Just tick the titles you want and fill in the form below. Prices and availability subject to change without notice.

Hodder Children's Books, Cash Sales Department, Bookpoint, 39 Milton Park, Abingdon, OXON, OX14 4TD, UK. If you have a credit card you may order by telephone. Our call centre team would be delighted to take your order. Our direct line is 01235 400414 (lines open 9.00 am – 6.00 pm Monday to Saturday, 24 hour message answering service). Alternatively you can send a fax on 01235 400454.

Please enclose a cheque or postal order made payable to Bookpoint Ltd to the value of the cover price and allow the following for postage and packing: UK & BFPO – £1.00 for the first book, 50p for the second book, and 30p for each additional book ordered up to a maximum charge of £3.00. OVERSEAS & EIRE – £2.00 for the first book, £1.00 for the second book, and 50p for each additional book.

Name...

Address...
....
If you would prefer to pay by credit card, please complete:

Please debit my Visa/ Access/ Diner's Club/ American Express (delete as applicable) card no:

Signature...

Expiry Date.......................................